TAKES CARE OF BUSINESS

created by

JAY ALBEE

raintree 🍂

a Capstone company — publishers for chii

Raintree is an imprint of Capstone Global Library Limited, a company incorporated in
England and Wales having its registered office at 264 Banbury Road, Oxford, OX2 7DY
– Registered company number: 6695582

www.raintree.co.uk
myorders@raintree.co.uk

Designed by Nathan Gassman

Special thanks to Manu Shadow Velasco for their consultation.

978 1 3982 5513 5

British Library Cataloguing in Publication Data
A full catalogue record for this book is available from the British Library.

Printed and bound in India.

CONTENTS

I'M RILEY!

I LOVE SO MANY THINGS! I LOVE CRAFTING.

THE ONLY THING BETTER THAN MAKING A MESS IS MAKING COOL STUFF.

I LOVE MY PARENTS, MY COUSINS AND MY FRIENDS.

I LOVE DOGS AND CATS . . .

AND BIRDS AND FISH . . .

AND DRAGONS AND UNICORNS AND ALL ANIMALS!

I'M NON-BINARY, AND I LOVE THAT TOO. I DON'T HAVE TO BE A BOY OR A GIRL.

I CAN JUST BE ME!

MX AUDE TEACHES HELPFUL TERMS

Cisgender: Cisgender (or cis) people identify with the gender written on their birth certificate. They are usually boys or girls.

Gender identity: Regardless of the gender on a person's birth certificate, they decide their gender identity. It might change over time. A person's interests, clothes and behaviour might be traditionally associated with their gender identity, or they might not.

Honorific: Young people use honorifics when they talk to or about adults, especially teachers. Mr is the honorific for a man, Mrs or Ms for a woman and Mx is the gender-neutral honorific often used for non-binary people. It is pronounced "mix". Non-binary people may also use Mr, Mrs or Ms.

LGBTQ+: This stands for lesbian, gay, bisexual (also pansexual), transgender, queer. There are lots of ways people describe their gender and attraction. These are just a few of those ways. The + sign means that there are many, many more, and they are all included in the acronym LGBTQ+.

Non-binary: Non-binary people have a gender identity other than boy or girl. They may be neither, both, a combination or sometimes one and sometimes the other.

Pronouns: Pronouns are how people refer to themselves and others (she/her, they/them, he/him, etc.). Pronouns often line up with gender identity (especially for cis people), but not always. It's best to ask a person what pronouns they like to use.

Queer: An umbrella term for people who identify as LGBTQ+.

Transgender: Transgender (or trans) people do not identify with the gender listed on their birth certificate. They might identify as the other binary gender, both genders

CHAPTER ONE

ALL ABOUT WALLACE

Everybody knew that Riley loved animals.

Sandy the tiny terrier across the street. Grandma Reynolds's grumpy cats. Abuelita's calm fish. Riley's best friend Lea's nervous guinea pig. Their other best friend Cricket's cheerful snake. Even Uncle Max's yappy Chihuahuas!

Riley loved every animal. But today was all about a dog so big and fluffy it was like a small bear. Today was all about Wallace!

Wallace was Cousin Matty's Bernese mountain dog crossed with a Saint Bernard. What's better than a big fluffy dog? Two kinds of big fluffy dogs in one!

This long weekend, Riley and their parents were house-sitting for their cousins. Or, as Riley thought of it, Mum and Dad were house-sitting. Riley was dog-sitting.

Cousin Matty had left Riley detailed instructions about how to look after Wallace properly for the next three days. Riley already knew them backwards and forwards.

Riley knew what to feed Wallace and when to walk him. They knew what kind of games he liked. They knew which sofas he was allowed to climb on and which ones he wasn't. Riley was all set.

Riley lay on the grass in Aunt Emma's big, pretty, fenced-in garden. But they weren't looking at the row of neat, big-headed roses along the fence or the poofy, even bigger-headed hydrangeas. They weren't looking at the pollinator patch, the herb patch or the petunia patch. They were entirely focused on Wallace, who lay near by.

The huge, old dog chewed a big bone propped between his front paws. He was entirely focused on the bone. Wallace paid no attention to Riley.

Looking at Wallace was great, but Riley really wanted to play. Wallace's toys were scattered all over the house. The garden too. Riley picked up a short, brightly coloured braided rope with two big knots at the ends. The slobbery bone dropped from Wallace's mouth. He looked at the rope. Then he looked at Riley.

It was often hard to tell how Wallace felt just by looking at him. He was an old dog now. His eyes were bright, but his droopy eyelids and jowls made him look bored. It wasn't until he wagged his tail that Riley was sure he was happy. His tail wagged now. Riley held out the braided rope.

Wallace stood up, stretched and chomped onto one of the knotted ends.

Riley tugged. Wallace clung to the rope. He moved his head casually from side to side. But such a big head and such a powerful jaw sent Riley jumping left and right. Riley held on tightly! They leaned back and held onto the rope with all their strength.

When Riley fell over backwards laughing, they declared Wallace the tug-of-war winner. The rope was covered in Wallace's slobber. So were Riley's hands!

"Eurgh!" Riley exclaimed.

They ran their hands through the dog's soft coat to wipe them off. Wallace seemed to enjoy the rub down, as he scruffed up his ears and snuffled.

"Consider this your reward for winning at tug-of-war," Riley said.

Matty's note said that even though Wallace had a big garden, he loved having two walks a day. He was clever, and clever dogs need to see and smell new things. Walks helped keep Wallace happy and active.

"What do you think, Wallace?" asked Riley. "Walk?"

Wallace showed instant excitement. His tail stuck straight out, as fluffy as an old-fashioned feather duster.

"Let's go!" said Riley.

The two dashed across the garden and into the house.

15

CAN'T KEEP AN
OLD DOG DOWN

"Dad!" Riley yelled into the house from the back door.

"Riley!" Dad yelled back. "Inside voice, please!"

Riley followed Dad's shout to the living room. Dad sat on a plush ottoman. He pointed a remote control at the huge, wall-mounted TV. He was talking to himself.

"A whole channel for Spanish-language cartoons!" He switched the channel. "A glass-blowing channel! All-day lawn bowling!" His glasses had slid down his long nose.

Riley loved it when Dad was super-focused on something. Riley squished onto the edge of the ottoman. Often, when they looked over Dad's shoulder, they knew exactly what he was excited about. At other times it was harder to tell. This was one of those times.

Dad laughed. "Celebrity dishwashing!"

"Dad, Wallace needs to go for a walk," said Riley.

"Okay, just give me a sec," said Dad, eyes locked on the screen. "There are so many channels. Look! Artisan ketchup making! Puppy Olympics! Alaskan penguin cam! I can't believe it!"

"Uh-oh," said Mum, coming into the room, sliding a bookmark into a new paperback novel. She swatted Dad lightly with the book. "Your concentration is pushing your glasses off your face."

Dad chuckled and pushed his glasses back up.

"Come on, Ry," Mum said. "I'll walk Wallace with you."

She threw the book onto one of the sofas. "You and me and Wallace makes three!" she sang, making up the tune as she went.

Riley jumped off the ottoman and looked around. "Where are you, Wallace? Wallace? Wally?"

Woof! Woof!

"Follow that bark," Riley said.

Riley and their mum found Wallace waiting by the front door. He sat with his head up, eyes locked on the doorknob.

"Someone's ready to go." Mum laughed as she put on her trainers.

From a hook by the door, Riley grabbed some poo bags and treats. They clipped Wallace's lead to his collar. Wallace stood up, wagged his tail and nudged his nose right up in the narrow space between the door and the doorframe. Mum opened the door. Wallace jumped outside with joy.

"He may be old, but sometimes he still behaves like a puppy!" Riley said.

CHAPTER THREE

IT'S WALLACE'S WORLD

Riley walked Wallace down the long driveway. The late summer afternoon breeze was warm. Riley felt as light as a feather. They made sure they had a good grip on Wallace's lead. Apart from Cousin Matty's note, Riley had grilled Cricket about his mum's dog and watched plenty of videos online.

Mum asked, "Did Matty's instructions say anything about Wallace's walks?"

"Oh, yeah." Riley knew it by heart. They ticked off all of Matty's important points. "He said that Wallace loves walks, but he can be slow. He said he'll want to smell everything. We can take our time. He's friendly with people and other dogs. It's okay if dogs want to play or people want to stroke him. He loves attention."

At the bottom of the driveway, Wallace turned left onto the pavement. Riley and Mum followed. Almost immediately, they met an elegant older man who held out a hand to Wallace. Wallace nuzzled into his hand like they had been friends forever.

"Nice to see you, Wallace," the man said. "Hello!" He waved to Riley and Mum as he walked past.

"Attention like that?" asked Mum.

"Just like that," said Riley. "Look at Wallace's tail go!"

Around the next corner, a woman walking her corgi stopped to let the two dogs sniff and play.

"Wallace is popular, isn't he?" Mum laughed.

"Everyone recognizes him," said Riley. "He's lived here all his life. It's like when we're walking along our street. We have to stop and say hello to Julia and Mr Arturo and everyone else who is out and about. This is Wallace's world, and we're just living in it for a few days."

"I think you're right," said Mum. Wallace made another turn, following his nose. "He certainly seems to know his way around."

They passed another person on the pavement, but they stepped onto the grass and kept their distance from Wallace.

"Matty said that some people might be scared of him. I think I get that. I mean, Wallace is huge. I might be scared of him if I met him for the first time."

Mum burst out laughing.

"What?" asked Riley.

"Ry, you have never been scared of Wallace." She took out her phone, quickly scrolled and showed them a photo. "Look."

While Wallace stopped for a good long sniff and snuffle at a tree, Riley took Mum's phone. She had pulled up a photo of Riley from years ago. In it, Riley, maybe one year old, was cuddled up to Wallace. They were both sleeping.

Riley laughed. "Wallace is twice the size of me!"

Mum laughed even more. "He always has been, even as a puppy."

Riley grinned and looked at the photo again. "He looks like he's wearing mittens four sizes too big for him."

Mum nodded. "They say that puppies grow into their paws. Little dogs have little paws. Puppies that are going to be big have paws like Wallace."

"I wonder if bear cubs have the same sized paws as puppy-Wallace? Can you take another photo of us?" asked Riley.

While Mum and Riley had talked, Wallace had circled the tree and found a knocked-over rubbish bin. He flopped over on his back and rubbed his fur through the rubbish.

And that's exactly what Riley and Mum saw when they looked up from the phone.

"Wallace! No!" yelled Riley.

"Get out of that," said Mum at the same time.

Wallace stood up and barked happily. He shook himself from head to tail. Bits of old spaghetti and orange peel flicked out of his fur.

"Eurgh," said Riley. "Wallace smells worse than Lea's guinea pig cage when she forgets to clean it."

Mum agreed and pinched her nose. "Worse than the stinkiest blue cheese," she said.

But Wallace didn't seem to mind. He trotted home with his tongue flopping and tail wagging the whole way.

29

CHAPTER FOUR

STINKY WALLACE

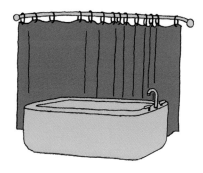

"We're back!" Riley called to Dad, kicking off their shoes.

Dad was right where they had left him. He still held the remote control, but his glasses were pushed onto the top of his head. "Vegetable lasagna," he said, perhaps to them, maybe to himself. "Horse bingo. Competitive jigsaw solving. Have you seen my glasses anywhere? I can't find them."

"They're on your head, Dad." Riley laughed.

Dad put his glasses back on his nose as he stretched and blinked. "How was walking Wallace?"

"Good," said Riley. "Not exactly what I expected."

Dad screwed up his nose. "Whoa! Something smells like Grandma Reynolds's cabbage surprise."

"It's Wallace," said Mum. "Riley, you'd better give him a bath."

"Matty's note didn't say anything about baths," said Riley. "But I did help Cricket give his mum's French bulldog a bath one time."

"Do you remember how you did it?" Mum asked.

"It was pretty easy. We got Tuffy into the bath, washed her and then dried her off. Come on, Wallace, off to the bathroom!" Riley said.

They ran to the bathroom with Wallace close behind. Riley laughed when they saw how big Wallace looked next to the bath.

"It's going to be a tight fit. Go on. Get in, Wallace," Riley said.

Riley bent over the edge of the bath and tapped the bottom.

"Come on," Riley said in a sing-songy voice.

Wallace didn't move.

Riley tugged his collar. They got behind him and pushed. Still nothing. They tried lifting his back legs, but Riley knew that was never going to work.

"Giving you a bath isn't going to be the same as giving Tuffy a bath, is it?" Riley said.

Riley thought for a moment. They remembered all the dog care videos they had watched. There were all kinds of ways to get a dog into a bath, and most of them included one thing . . .

"Treats!" Riley said.

They dashed out of the room and came back with a bag of chewy dog snacks. Wallace perked up when he saw them. Riley held up a treat.

"Wallace. Get in the bath," Riley said.

Riley couldn't tell whether Wallace didn't understand or just didn't want to do it. Either way, Riley was going to have to make this work.

Riley dropped the treat into the bath and said, "Get it, Wallace!"

Wallace understood that! He threw one huge paw into the bath, snapped up the treat, and was back on the bath mat in the blink of an eye. Wallace licked his chops and barked happily.

Riley put a treat at the far end of the bath. Wallace would have to climb all the way in to get it – or so they thought.

Instead, Wallace barged past Riley, bumped them out of the way, put one paw in the tub, chomped, and was back on the mat.

Riley huffed a little in frustration. They climbed into the bath and shoved the treats into their pocket. They turned on the tap and splashed around a little.

"Oooh! That's nice!" Riley said in their best sing-songy voice. "I think you'd really like it in here, Wallace!" They clapped their hands. "I think you really, really would."

Wallace's tail wagged. Riley was on the right track! They squeezed a blob of Wallace's shampoo onto their hands and lathered up.

"Wow, being clean feels so nice," Riley said.

They held out a hand to Wallace so he could smell the soap. But Wallace was more interested in sniffing Riley's pocket and the hidden treats.

"Come on, buddy. Come on in. I'll give you all the treats you want if you get in here," Riley said.

Wallace sat on the bath mat.

Dad poked his head around the bathroom door. "How're you doing in here?" He grinned. "Wait. I thought it was Wallace who rolled in the rubbish, not you!"

"Very funny, Dad," said Riley. "I saw a video of someone doing this to get a dog in a bath. It's not working on Wallace though."

"I doubt we can make Wallace do anything he doesn't want to do. Time to think outside the box," he said. "Or, in this case, outside the bath!"

CHAPTER FIVE

STINKIER WALLACE

"Come with me," Dad said.

Riley and Wallace followed him to the garden shed. A large, blue plastic paddling pool hung on one wall.

"Ta-da!" said Dad.

Riley's eyes went wide. "Wow! Great idea, Dad!"

Dad and Riley carried the paddling pool through the garden and put it down by the patio. Wallace lay near by with his head resting on his paws. Dad uncoiled the garden hose.

"It's got a fancy nozzle," said Dad, handing it to Riley. "Hold it here and twist the head to change the water flow."

"Fun!" said Riley.

They clicked the head from shower spray to hose-style flow and more. Wallace lifted himself up. He sniffed at the paddling pool and lapped at the water.

"That's it, Wallace! Get in the pool," Riley said.

"I'm still not a hundred per cent sure how we get him to do that," admitted Dad.

Riley clicked through different sprays.

Dad was still thinking about TV.

"You know, I found a pottery channel. I worked out how to record the international pottery championship live from Sweden at three a.m. So, that's something to look forward to tomorrow," he said.

"Cool," said Riley, still playing with the fancy nozzle.

Riley clicked to the choppy, broken *ch-ch-ch* flow. Wallace's tail wagged. He leaped into the pool with a splash and tried to bite the stream.

"Whoa!" said Riley.

"Wow!" Dad exclaimed. "Problem solved, I guess! Try to get him wet all over."

Riley laughed as they jumped around the pool, trying to get the spray on Wallace's back. Wallace was jumping around too so he could chomp the water.

Riley took the bag from their pocket and held it out to Dad. "I think he deserves some treats!"

Dad held out a treat to Wallace, who was delighted to have snacks and the *ch-ch-ch* water.

"Riley!" said Dad. "Try not to get me as wet as Wallace!"

"Sorry," Riley said.

Mum came into the garden with a tray of marinated steaks. Mum and Dad loved cooking outside. At home, they used a little portable grill. It was all that would fit in their garden. But the cousins' barbecue was a huge, shiny thing with all kinds of knobs and settings.

"I am going to cook up a storm!" said

Mum. She pressed a button or two. "Or I will if I can work out how to light this thing."

The paddling pool was finally full, and Wallace was wet from head to tail.

From the barbecue, Mum gave a huff.

"I can't turn this fancy thing on," Mum said.

Dad went over. "Hmm. I think you just . . ." He trailed off as he pushed the same buttons Mum had tried.

Riley squirted a big blob of shampoo on Wallace's back. By the time Riley had put the bottle down, Wallace was halfway out of the pool.

"Wallace! Stop!" said Riley, lunging at the dog. "Dad! The treats!"

"Oh!" blurted out Dad, as Wallace

rushed past him to roll around in the grass, right past the treat in Dad's outstretched hand.

"Bathing Wallace is nothing like bathing Tuffy," Riley said. "But at least he got the shampoo off."

"Maybe give him a final rinse anyway," said Dad. "It can't hurt."

Riley found a dense flow from the nozzle. "Come here, Wallace. Stay still!" they said, chasing him around the garden with the hose.

"Ha!" said Mum in triumph. "It's lit!"

"Ha!" said Riley, shutting off the hose. "He's rinsed!"

With the game of run-away-from-the-hose over, Wallace trotted over to Dad and gently took the treat he was still holding. Then he shook himself from the tip of his nose to the tip of his tail. Water sprayed everywhere – all over Mum, Dad and the barbecue!

Mum and Dad gasped at the cold water. The barbecue made a sizzling noise and went out. Wallace's tail was wagging and all three of the Reynolds were soaked.

Suddenly, Mum burst out laughing. It was too ridiculous not to. Dad and Riley had to laugh too.

"Pizza for dinner?" asked Mum.

That night, half-stinky Wallace slept in the laundry room.

45

WALLACE AND HIS HAPPY PLACE

In the morning, Riley let Wallace out of the laundry room and fed him breakfast.

"Ugh," said Riley. "He still smells bad."

"Something else that stinks," said Dad, slowly stirring his coffee, "is that I didn't record the international pottery championship. I got *A Quilter's Journey of Scotland* instead."

"I'm sorry," said Mum. "I'm sure you'll be able to find it later online."

"That's true," said Dad, brightening up. He took a big bite of his toast. "You know, I think I know what I might have done wrong. I'll try again. There's this other channel I was looking at . . ."

After breakfast, Riley and Mum walked Wallace to the dog park. It was the kind of late summer day when you could feel autumn coming. Riley kept a close eye on Wallace, making sure he didn't find any more smelly things to roll in.

"I want to try washing Wallace again today," said Riley. "He still smells."

"He's pretty funky," agreed Mum. "Like when we came back from holiday and the milk had gone off."

"Like when Dad left that fish in the fridge too long," agreed Riley.

"Worse than your trainers at the end of term!" Mum laughed. "Dad and I will help this time. And I want to try that barbecue again. I stayed up late reading the user manual and some tips online. It's even more complicated than the TV!"

At the dog park, Riley led Wallace through the two gates to the big dog area. Mum made sure the gates were closed securely behind them. Riley unclipped Wallace's lead. It was like Riley had hit his "GO!" button.

Wallace bounded to the far end of the enclosure, cut sharply behind a bench and bounded back. He skidded behind Riley and took off again. You aren't allowed in a dog run unless you have a dog. Being inside the fence was different from peering through it.

Wallace was the biggest dog in the park. As he galloped around, dogs ran with him, the way fish might swim along with a whale. A fluffy Australian shepherd nipped his ears. A sleek Weimaraner puppy jumped up at him. A zippy terrier ducked through his legs and zoomed under his tummy.

It was just like walking in Wallace's street. Plenty of people and dogs recognized him, and he seemed happy to see all of them. This was Wallace's happy place.

Wallace flopped over and rubbed his back on the ground. Riley and Mum laughed as three dogs jumped on his belly. His tongue lolled and he grinned.

When Wallace was worn out, he flopped onto the ground in front of Riley and Mum's bench. Dogs continued to jump all over him. He played with them but stayed lying down.

People and dogs came and went. A poodle trotted in and made straight for Wallace. Wallace jumped up. The poodle's owner gave Wallace a big smile.

"Hi, Wallace!" she said.

The poodle's owner sat with Mum and Riley while the two dogs frolicked about.

"You must be Matt's cousins! He told me you were Wallace-sitting this weekend," she said. "I'm Tina. That's Pixie."

"I'm Riley."

"Nice to meet you," said Mum.

"How's it going so far?" asked Tina.

"Pretty good," said Riley. "But it is so much more work than I thought it would be."

Tina laughed. "Looking after a big dog is big work," she said. "Even other dog owners don't really get it. Like, how big the poos can get."

"No kidding!" Mum laughed.

"Can I say hello to Pixie?" asked Riley, knowing it was polite to always ask to stroke a dog. "Yes, she loves meeting new people," said Tina.

"Her coat is so soft," said Riley.

"She had a bath yesterday. She was a total mess before that," Tina said.

"I gave Wallace a bath yesterday too," said Riley. "Well, a half-bath. He wouldn't stay still so I couldn't lather him up. That's why he still smells."

"Did you run out of peanut butter?" asked Tina.

She threw Pixie's ball and the poodle, Wallace and a cocker spaniel all took off after it.

"What's peanut butter for?" Riley asked.

"Most dogs will do anything for peanut butter. They love it. Put some on a spoon or your finger and he'll lick it off bit by bit. That's how I can bathe Pixie. Or trim her nails or brush her. Really, any grooming she isn't into," Tina said.

"You know, I wondered why there was a giant jar of peanut butter in the cupboard with Wallace's shampoo. I'm going to try it! Thanks, Tina!" Riley beamed.

CHAPTER SEVEN

PEANUT BUTTER TO THE RESCUE

Straight away, Riley could tell that the second attempt at bathing Wallace would be better. Firstly, Wallace was worn out from the dog park. He didn't want to leap around and bite at the water. Secondly, Mum and Dad were helping. And thirdly, Riley had peanut butter.

Wallace stood in the paddling pool. He licked peanut butter off a wooden spoon while Mum and Dad quickly rubbed shampoo through his coat.

"It's working," said Riley.

Even with his huge tongue, Wallace took lots of licks to clean the spoon. His tail wagged. His jowls swung as he worked the sticky peanut butter around in his mouth. He told Riley he was ready for more by trying to shove his snout in the jar.

"Keep him busy, Ry," said Mum. "We have to rinse him off."

Dad ran the hose over Wallace's back and under his tummy. They had to be thorough or he would still smell. "His coat is so thick!"

"Oh, no!" yelled Riley. "He pulled the spoon right out of my hands!"

"Keep feeding him," Mum said. "We've almost finished."

"Wallace's drool is thicker than ever! He's trying to get the bits of peanut butter from between my fingers," Riley said.

"Okay," said Dad, turning off the hose. "Towel time."

Mum and Dad fluffed Wallace all over with thick towels. And that was it! Wallace was finally clean!

"We did it!" said Mum.

Riley's hand dripped with goopy slobber. "It took all three of us and lots of peanut butter, but we did it."

"Peanut butter," marvelled Dad. "I never would have guessed."

Mum pulled out her phone and took some photos. They were mostly of Riley trying to stop Wallace putting his whole head in the peanut butter jar.

Mum grilled the steaks and some vegetables on the barbecue. They then ate them in the garden, soaking in the last of the summer sun. Wallace gobbled up strips of steak but was less enthusiastic about aubergine and peppers. After all the activity of the day, Riley thought that it was nice to relax.

When the air cooled and the sun went behind the clouds, they all went inside.

"I was thinking," said Dad. "That quilters' Scottish tour show might actually be interesting."

"Put it on," encouraged Mum.

Mum and Dad sat on the big sofa. Dad pushed his glasses onto his head and flipped through menus on the TV.

Wallace jumped up into the small space between them and shuffled them to the edges of the sofa. He stretched out, his head on Mum's lap and his wagging tail thumping on Dad's knees.

Riley sat right in the middle of the sofa, leaning against Wallace's tummy. They moved gently up and down as Wallace breathed in and out.

"I can't find the quilting show," Dad said, squinting at the remote. "But I did find chainsaw ice sculpting!"

"That's just fine." Mum chuckled. "Ry, remember the ice sculpture we saw last winter?"

But Riley and Wallace were already asleep – a well-earned rest after such a busy summer weekend.

THE END

DISCUSSION QUESTIONS

1. At the dog park, poodle owner Tina tells Riley that dogs love peanut butter. Without that tip, what other things could Riley have tried when bathing Wallace?

2. In the story, Riley, Mum and Dad all have something that goes wrong. Why do you think it's important that they each tried again?

3. Riley watched lots of videos and talked to their friends about dogsitting. Do you think that was a good way to prepare? Why or why not?

WRITING PROMPTS

1. Riley was surprised at how much work it was to look after a big dog. Write about a time when you were surprised by something.

2. People aren't allowed inside a dog park if they don't have a dog. Write about a place you aren't normally allowed to be in. What would it feel like to be there?

3. Cousin Matty tells Riley that not everyone will want to stroke Wallace because some people might be afraid of him. Write about a fear you have and what you do to manage it.

MEET THE CREATORS

Jay Albee is the joint pen name for LGBTQ+ couple Jen Breach and J. Anthony. Between them, they've done lots of jobs: archaeologist, illustrator, ticket taker and bagel baker, but now they write and draw all day long in their house in Philadelphia, USA.

Sometimes they dog-sit a handsome dog called Spatula.

Jen Breach

J. Anthony